Why
She Went
Home

1. *She hated her job*

2. *Her apartment depressed her*

3. *Yet another relationship had failed to live up to its promise of everlasting love*

4. *Therapy had become a prison from which she saw no escape*

5. *Where once they'd been vaguely irritating I's, all her old friends had lately turned into extremely wearying we's*

6. *She was tired of trying (and failing) to be someone*

7. *She was drinking heavily*

8. *She actually missed New Jersey*

9. *Images of sneaker-sized water bugs haunted her dreams and waking thoughts alike*

10. *Her mother was ill*

Praise for *Why She Went Home*

"Ebullient yet deeply moving . . . highly original . . . In its exploration of how small-town American life and humdrum family drama can become operatic in theme, *Why She Went Home* has more in common with Philip Roth and early Updike than it does with Helen Fielding and Melissa Banks. Rosenfeld explores this territory with a uniquely feminine eye."   —*Vogue*

"As always, Rosenfeld has a wonderful eye for detail. . . . Her portrait of the multiclass, multiethnic Jersey mall-scape is spot on."

—*The New York Times Book Review*

"Smart, funny . . . chick lit—but with the emphasis on *lit*."   —*Glamour*

"[Rosenfeld's] two novels succeed in capturing the pain and the humor of being almost adult. . . . *Why She Went Home* . . . manages to be both hilariously funny and poignant. Rosenfeld has a sharp, original, daring comic voice. . . . Refreshingly unsentimental . . . Honest, eccentric, likable, and witty, much like its heroine."

—*Boston Sunday Globe*

"There's something terribly refreshing about an almost-thirty heroine who prefers an evening sitting in her parents' run-down, fluorescently lit New Jersey kitchen munching on oat-bran flakes to 'Sex in the City'–style party-hopping around lower Manhattan. . . . Rosenfeld doesn't skimp on details either, which is part of her charm."   —*The Washington Post Book World*

"Funny, sassy . . . Rosenfeld's style is witty and winning."
—*Publishers Weekly*

"Captivating . . . Twenty- and thirtysomethings . . . will relate to [Phoebe's] struggles in this charming, often hilarious novel."
—*Booklist*

"Like [*What She Saw* . . . , Rosenfeld's] first novel, *Why She Went Home* is both funny and affecting, thanks to Rosenfeld's keen ear for the 'strings of cliches' and 'blatant failures of language' that dog most relationships."
—*Village Voice*

"Freshly handled . . . The characters are original and touching. This novel's dialogue, its reversals of fortune, and, of course, its love-match ending, are all deliciously satisfying and . . . snortingly funny."
—*Organic Style*

"Once again author Lucinda Rosenfeld has absolutely nailed it. . . . We'll just slurp this one up and wait for the next installment of the Very Fine Phoebe Chronicles."
—*Daily Candy NYC*

"Funny and loveable, the Fines will have you grinning through it all."
—*Lifetime Magazine*

"Who knew that a voice this hysterically funny could render family life with such sadness and depth. By the fifth page, I was ready to follow Lucinda Rosenfeld's heroine to hell and back, not to mention her native New Jersey. Take this book home with you!"

—GARY SHTEYNGART,
author of *The Russian Debutante's Handbook*